Birthday Cookies

by Julie Verne

illustrated by Len Ebert

Harcourt

Orlando   Boston   Dallas   Chicago   San Diego

Visit *The Learning Site!*

www.harcourtschool.com

59611

"Today is Mama's birthday.
Papa always makes a yellow
cake for Mama," said Marco.

"Papa is sick today," said Tina.
"What can we do?"

"How do you make a yellow
cake?" asked Tina. "The recipe
looks hard."

"Let's make cookies!" said Tina.
"Henry can help us."

Marco and Tina poured and
mixed. The cookie dough was
thicker than cake batter.

They tasted the buttery dough.
"Mmm! It's perfect!"

They put the cookie dough
on cookie sheets. They cleaned
up the dough that was smeared
everywhere.

"Mama is 40 today, so we need to make 40 cookies," said Tina. "Let's make one more for good luck," said Marco.

Henry helped them bake the cookies. When they were cool, Marco and Tina frosted them.

"These cookies look so good!"
said Marco. "I can't wait to
taste one."

"Help me count the cookies," said Tina. "We have 10, 20, 30, 40, 41 cookies," said Marco.

"Mama will be surprised to see so many cookies. She will be surprised that we made them," said Marco.

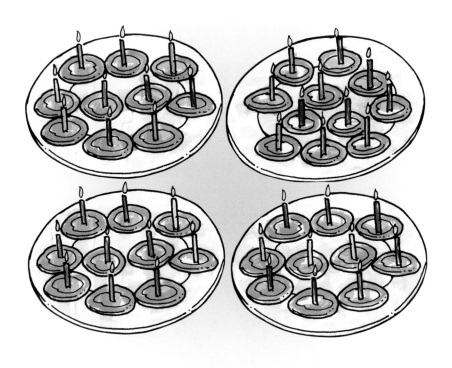

The children took the cookies
to show Papa. Then Henry lit a
candle on each cookie.

They called Mama into the
bedroom. Everyone sang
"Happy Birthday" as she walked
in. Then Mama blew out the
candles.

"Look at these cookies!" she said. "There are 10, 20, 30, 40, 41 of them. What a wonderful surprise from my wonderful children."